Clown

by Liza Charlesworth

ISBN: 978-1-338-78290-5
Illustrated by John Lund
Copyright © 2021 by Liza Charlesworth. All rights reserved.
Published by Scholastic Inc., 557 Broadway, New York, NY 10012

10 9 8 7 6 5 4 3 2 1   68   21 22 23 24 25 26 27/0

Printed in Jiaxing, China. First printing, June 2021.

Look at the clown car!
Their car can drive.

Look at the clown car!
Their car can float.

3

Look at the clown car!
Their car can dive.

Look at the clown car!
Their car can fly.

Look at the clown car!
Their car can catch.

Look at the clown car!
Their car can walk.

Look at the clown car!
Their car can talk.